S0-CPF-424

ARTHUR ASHE

Champion of Dreams and Motion

By Stuart A. Kallen

3000300030 0041

95-69

Published by Abdo & Daughters, 4940 Viking Drive Suite 622, Edina, Minnesota 55435.

Library bound edition distributed by Rockbottom Books, Pentagon Tower, P.O. Box 36036, Minneapolis, Minnesota 55435.

Copyright ©1993 by Abdo Consulting Group, Inc., Pentagon Tower, P.O. Box 36036, Minneapolis, Minnesota 55435. International copyrights reserved in all countries. No part of this book may be reproduced without written permission from the copyright holder. Printed in the U.S.A.

Interior photographs: Bettmann Archive
Cover photo: UPI Bettman

Edited by Rosemary Wallner

Library of Congress Cataloging-in-publication Data

Kallen, Stuart A., 1955-
    Arthur Ashe : Champion of Dreams and Motion / by Stuart A. Kallen.
        p.   cm. -- (I Have a Dream)
    Includes index and glossary (p.)
    ISBN 1-56239-255-7
    1. Ashe, Arthur -- juvenile literature. 2. Tennis players -- United States -- Biography -- juvenile literature.   I. Title. II. Series.
GV994.A7K35   1993
796.342'092--dc20
[B]   93-8623
                                          CIP
                                          AC

TABLE OF CONTENTS

Chapter 1 - Playing to Win **4**

Serving at Six 6

Picked by the Pros 7

Tennis Heaven 9

Number Five in the Nation 11

Chapter 2 - College Champ **14**

The Road to Wimbledon 15

On to the Davis Cup 17

Chapter 3 -Top Ranked **18**

Second Lieutenant Ashe 19

Bringing Home the Davis Cup 22

Chipping Away at Racism 23

Chapter 4 - Wimbledon and Beyond **28**

Tennis the Menace 30

Hobbling Down the Aisle 31

The Fight of His Life 31

Life After Tennis 34

Struck Down by AIDS 35

Glossary **39**

Index **40**

Chapter 1

Playing

to

Win

The crowd at Wimbledon was going wild. Two tennis players were locked in a tense battle of skill and strategy. Arthur Ashe and his opponent Jimmy Connors were a blur of arms and legs, smashing volley after volley with their tennis rackets. Ashe seemed to leap from one end of the court to another. Connors was starting to wear down. Someone in the crowd yelled, "Come on, Connors!" The angry Connors yelled back, "I'm trying, for crisake!" Ashe kept feeding him junk shots, forcing him to net and lob.

Finally there was a break in the action. All eyes were on Ashe, resting in his chair. He was peering mysteriously into his cupped hands. The crowd thought he might be praying. In reality, Ashe was reading notes he had prepared for the game. He had made notes on small cards to remind him to follow through with his pre-planned strategy. While the crowd sat on the edges of their chairs with excitement, the mild-mannered Ashe was studying.

Arthur Ashe learned to play tennis on playgrounds similiar to this one. Ashe held tennis clinics for under-privileged youths in Washington D.C.

The match resumed and Ashe stuck to his plan. He would tire Connors with junk shots. After several more games, Ashe drove home an overhead smash and won the championship trophy at Wimbledon. The 32-year-old Arthur Ashe was the first African-American man to win such an honor. As he held the trophy over his head for the cameras and the crowd, Arthur Ashe was at the peak of his power.

SERVING AT SIX

Arthur Robert Ashe, Jr., was born in Richmond, Virginia, on July 10, 1943. Until he was four years old, he lived with his parents, Arthur, Sr., and Mattie, at his uncle's house in Richmond's African-American district. In 1947, the city of Richmond hired Arthur's father as a special police officer in charge of Brookfield Playground, an 18-acre park. As one of the job benefits, the Ashe family got to live in a five-room house inside the park. Brookfield was the largest blacks-only playground in the city. It had an Olympic-size swimming pool, basketball courts, baseball diamonds, and four hard-surface tennis courts. To Arthur, living in the middle of this athlete's paradise was a dream come true.

Arthur said that he was as skinny as a "soda straw." Still, he began swinging the tennis racket by the age of six. He had extra-quick reflexes and soon everybody noticed the little boy who could play tennis.

Living in the middle of a huge park would tempt most children to ignore their studies. But Arthur's mother taught him to read even before he entered school. Arthur fondly remembered many days where he would do nothing but listen to soft music and read. He always got straight A's and was elected class president in sixth grade.

Arthur was kept busy with more than tennis and reading. His father was very kind, but strict with his children. Arthur and his younger brother Johnny, born in 1948, were expected home exactly ten minutes after school let out. Then they would help with chores, which included taking care of Brookfield. In this manner, Arthur and Johnny learned a lot about how the park was run.

Life was good for young Arthur until one horrible day in March 1950. Mattie Ashe checked into the hospital for minor surgery. After the operation, problems developed and Mattie died. Arthur was crushed.

After Mattie's death, Arthur's father hired Mrs. Otis Berry, an elderly widow, to take care of the children. Arthur had a difficult time accepting this kind woman as a substitute mother. Five years later Arthur's father married Lorene Kimbrough. She moved in with her two children. This prompted Mrs. Berry to move into the room shared by Arthur and Johnny. It was an awkward situation, two young boys sharing a room with an older woman. But Arthur wasn't around much. He was down on the tennis courts practicing his backstroke.

PICKED BY THE PROS

*A*s a child, Arthur was hardly the picture of a professional athlete. He had a host of childhood diseases including whooping cough, chicken pox, diphtheria, measles, and mumps. All the sicknesses left him weak and thin. Because of this, Arthur could not compete in most sports. He felt his abilities would only be recognized in baseball and tennis.

During Arthur's childhood in the city of Richmond, and the South in general, African-Americans were not allowed to use the same facilities as white people. Black people had their own schools, hospitals, restaurants, and parks. On buses and trains, black people were forced to sit in separate sections, labeled "colored only." ("Colored" is a term used for African-Americans before the 1960s) Most of the time, the "colored only" sections were kept broken down and dirty by the white people who were in charge of them. There was segregation, or separation, of the races, in everything from barbershops to sports arenas. Where Arthur lived, there was a "colored only" playground. Most of the other facilities were for "whites only." If African-Americans tried to use "whites-only" facilities, they could be arrested.

But Arthur's love of tennis crossed all color lines. Sometimes he would watch white kids playing at Byrd Park, where it was illegal for him to set foot. The more he watched, the more he learned and the more he loved the game. But Arthur probably never would have become a tennis pro if it weren't for Ronald Charity. A student at the nearby University Union of Virginia, Charity was one of America's top black tennis players. He had taught himself the game with several how-to books and a borrowed racket. In the summer, Charity taught tennis at Brookfield.

Arthur used to watch Charity polish his strokes for hours. One day, Charity offered to show seven-year-old Arthur the game. Charity was impressed with Arthur's willingness to learn. He began spending hours with the young boy showing him the proper grip, forehand and backhand shots, and correcting his stroke. Arthur also practiced for hours when by himself.

Soon Arthur was competing with boys several years older than himself—and winning. By the time he was 10, he was playing with grown-ups at Richmond Racquet Club. Arthur's talents were so obvious that Charity decided he needed a better coach.

Arthur began playing under the watchful eye of Dr. Robert Walter Johnson. A successful medical doctor, Johnson was also an avid player. He had a court in his backyard, and played at national championships with tennis great Althea Gibson, the first female African-American tennis champion.

After Johnson retired from competition, he decided to promote tennis among young African-Americans. Each summer, he took promising young black tennis players into his home and coached them on the fine points of the game. He also took them on the road to play tournaments. He called these players his Junior Development Team. Since most of the players came from poor families, Johnson paid all their expenses.

In the spring of 1953, the Central Intercollegiate Athletic Association, a organization of black colleges, held a tennis tournament at Virginia Union University. During a break between matches, Charity introduced Arthur to Johnson. After watching the soon-to-be ten-year-old hit some balls, Johnson agreed to take Arthur to his house in Lynchburg for two weeks.

TENNIS HEAVEN

*J*ohnson's home was tennis heaven. There was a service stand for holding a ball in place while practicing strokes. There was a ball hanging on a cord in the garage where budding tennis players could hit the ball with a racket-length broom handle. And there was a ball-spitting Ball-Boy machine. Arthur would rise at six in the morning in order to practice 45 minutes before breakfast.

Arthur's days were filled with drills made up of every kind of tennis shot—cross-court, down the line, forehand deep, forehand approach, return of serve, and backhand shots. Johnson made all his students hit each shot 100 times in a row.

When he wasn't practicing tennis, Arthur was reading about it. Johnson's library had dozens of books on tennis strategy. Because he was not as big as the other players, Arthur realized that a good game plan was as important as physical strength. Arthur learned to become a tough, consistent player. By keeping the ball in play with a mind towards tiring his opponent, Arthur conserved his strength until his opponent made a mistake. In this way Arthur was able to outlast his competitors by watching from the baseline.

Johnson also taught his players manners. Anxious to prove the skill of his black players in a white tennis world, Johnson wanted to avoid racial conflict. Johnson taught the Junior Development Team to keep their cool when angry and never argue with an umpire's call. And manners extended off the court. When the team traveled they were expected to be perfect ladies and gentlemen at all times. Throughout his career, Arthur carried these lessons with him. He was almost as famous for his emotional control as he was for his game.

That summer at Johnson's home was the first of many for Arthur. He headed there every summer until he was 18 years old. And the practice paid off. The second summer at Johnson's, Arthur won the 12-and-under division of every tournament he entered. In 1957 and 1958, Arthur won the American Tennis Associations (ATA) National Championship for boys. (The ATA was the African-American tennis organization.)

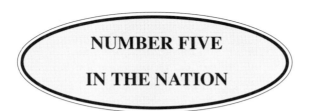

When he was 15, Arthur reached the semifinals of the mostly white New Jersey Boy's Tournament. He also topped a field of 150 white players in the Maryland Junior Tournament. But when he tried to compete in his hometown's U. S. Lawn Tennis Association (USLTA) tournament, he was refused because he was black. Arthur took some comfort in the fact that the USLTA, while denying him equal rights, still ranked him as fifth among all the boys in the country. He had also beat his mentor, Ronald Charity in an ATA tournament. In 1960, Arthur won the ATA's junior's and men's singles titles, becoming that tournament's youngest champion ever.

If Arthur was going to continue his progress, he needed to leave Richmond. He could not play in the winter because no indoor courts were opened to blacks. And there was no one to compete with in Virginia. Arthur was so good that no one else could come close to his level of skill. With this in mind, Arthur father sent him to Sumner High School in St. Louis, Missouri. There, he practiced indoors in the winter and competed against champs like Cliff and Butch Buchholz and Chuck McKinley.

The move was a great for Arthur's game. When he played indoors at the 138th Infantry Armory, the wooden floors encouraged him to develop a more aggressive style. With the help of local pro Larry Miller, Arthur learned to shorten his backswing, rush the net more often, and add some sizzle to his serve.

Arthur Ashe of Sumner High School, shown here winning the
National Interscholastic Tennis Championship in 1961.

With his excellent record in sports, Arthur's classmates treated him like a star. During the Christmas break, J. D. Morgan, coach of the men's tennis team at the University of California, Los Angeles (UCLA), called Arthur. Morgan offered Arthur an athletic scholarship to the university, and Arthur accepted. By the end of the year, Arthur graduated with the highest grade point average in his high school. This guy was going somewhere.

Tennis star Arthur Ashe in action at the U.S. Open.

Chapter **2**

College

Champ

J.D. Morgan had first seen Arthur Ashe play in the National Boys Championship in Kalamazoo, Michigan, in 1958. Since then, he had kept an eye on Ashe's developing talent. He offered Ashe the scholarship at the end of 1960. It was the first time the school had made such an offer to an African-American tennis player.

But Ashe had received many offers at that point. Hampton Institute, the University of Arizona, and the University of Michigan were all making offers to Ashe. But UCLA had the top tennis program in the nation. Ashe had no trouble making up his mind. Moments into his first conversation with Morgan, Ashe told him, "Don't worry, I'll be there."

College was nine months away. In the meantime, Ashe won his second major title, the National Interscholastics. He reached the semifinals of the National Jaycees and National Juniors tournaments. Ashe became the fifth-ranked junior in America and was a member of the U.S. Junior Davis Cup team. He also won both the ATA's singles and doubles (with Ronald Charity) titles. In a day when teenagers did not dominate the tennis scene as they do today, Ashe was the 28th-ranked amateur in the nation.

When it was time to go to the university, Ashe was ready to close a chapter in his life. He wrote in his 1981 book *Off the Court*, "When I decided to leave Richmond, I decided to leave all that Richmond stood for at that time—its segregation, its conservatism, its parochial thinking, its slow progress toward equality, its lack of opportunity for talented black people. I had no intention of coming back."

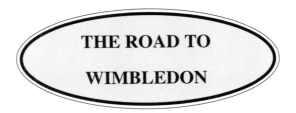

THE ROAD TO WIMBLEDON

*A*t UCLA, Ashe's days were filled with a whirlwind of classes, tennis, and work. Playing tennis on the top university team was a new experience for Ashe. He was used to being the top player at any match. But his teammates at UCLA were some of the best in the nation. Still, Ashe started a respectable number three behind Charlie Pasarell, the National Juniors champion, and Dave Reed, who held the Southern California juniors title. Ashe thrived on the competition, playing on the UCLA Bruins against some of the top juniors in the world. This was high-level competition for the first time in his life.

Although far away from the segregation of Virginia, Ashe was still forced to face prejudice. When the Balboa Bay Club in Orange County hosted a tournament of college teams, Ashe wasn't invited because he was black. Charlie Pasarell offered to boycott the tournament as a show of support for Ashe. Coach Morgan offered to keep the entire UCLA team out as an act of protest. But Ashe preferred not to make waves. This incident made Ashe realize that he had strong allies in his teammates and coach. Several years later, when Ashe was famous, the Balboa Bay Club invited him to their tournaments every year. Ashe refused them every time.

Meanwhile, Arthur Ashe was becoming a tennis star. During his sophomore year, he won the Southern California sectional title and with it, an automatic entry into the singles draw at the All-England Championships at Wimbledon. This made Ashe one of only 128 men worldwide to receive such an honor.

The All-England Lawn Tennis and Croquet Club in the London suburb of Wimbledon has been the mecca for tennis players for more than 100 years. The first lawn-tennis tournaments in history were held there in 1877. That was only four years after the sport was invented in Wales by Major Walter Clopton Wingfield. (Wingfield adapted the sport from the 700-year-old game of court tennis.) Since then, every one of the sport's greatest players has played there.

The tournament at Wimbledon is bound in tradition. All matches are held on grass courts, just as they were in Major Wingfield's day. The players are expected to dress in white outfits. And each player that enters and exits the club's main stadium—Centre Court—must bow or curtsy before the Royal Box. This is where the British royalty sit. For nearly 100 years, most of the players who played at Wimbledon were white and upper class.

The trip to England was like a dream. When Ashe arrived in London, a Bentley limousine was waiting for him at the airport. Each day, the car took him from his hotel to the All-England Lawn Tennis and Croquet Club for each match. Ashe later recalled: "The umpires wore hard straw hats and carnations just as they did in 1880. There was green every-where—green ivy, green canopies, green doors and balconies and chairs.... All the magnificence and efficiency dazed me a little."

While Ashe may have been dazed by all the green, when it came time to play tennis, he was a strong opponent. He beat his first two adversaries, finally losing to Chuck McKinley, who was America's top player at the time.

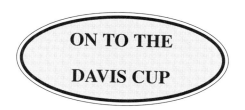

ON TO THE DAVIS CUP

*A*fter Wimbledon, Ashe reached the semifinals at a tournament in Budapest, Hungry. On the way home he lost five sets in Denmark's Torben Ulrich. When he returned from his European matches, his standing had improved. When he started at UCLA, he was the 28th-ranked amateur. Now he was number six.

When Ashe returned home, his put his bullet-fast serve and incredible backhand to work at the U.S. Hardcourt Championship in Chicago. His victory in Chicago helped him win a place on the U.S. Davis Cup squad.

The Davis Cup competition pits country against country. Each nation seeks to fill the squad with its finest players. Ashe felt that not only was it an honor, but his patriotic duty to play for the United States. After beating Venezuela's top player in the first match, Ashe had to quit the team to complete his junior year.

After finishing the school year, Ashe honed his skills again at Wimbledon and the U.S. National Championships. He won some and he lost some, but he finished 1964 with a crowning achievement. Ashe was awarded the Johnson Award, given each year to the tennis player who contributes the most to the sport. Winners must also show good sportsmanship and character. Not only was the award an honor to Ashe, but it also showed that the wealthy, all-white country club set had finally accepted an African-American athlete. By the end of the year, Arthur Ashe was the third-ranked player in the United States.

Chapter **3**

Top
Ranked

In 1965 Arthur Ashe was asked again to play on the U.S. Davis Cup team. By the end of the school year he won the NCAA singles title and captured the doubles title. At the age of 21, he was the top collegiate player in the nation. He continued his hot streak with decent showings at Wimbledon and on the Davis Cup team.

At the U.S. Nationals in Forest Hills, New York, Ashe squared off against Roy Emerson, the top-ranked amateur player in the world. Ashe was not expected to do much more than put up a good fight. But by using his well-known strategy of calm self-discipline, Ashe faced down Emerson's aggressive assault to win. The story of Ashe's surprise victory made the front page of Richmond's *News Leader.* Ashe was walking on air after defeating Emerson. He said: "Naturally I hit the trail harder now. I was like a hunting dog that sniffs something good. Beating Emerson showed me that I might be able to lick anybody in the wide world."

In the spring of 1966, Ashe graduated from UCLA. The city of Richmond decided to show to their now-famous native son. February 4, 1966, was declared Arthur Ashe Day. Ashe stayed in the city's finest hotel. He was honored at a banquet attended by the mayor and other politicians. Ronald Charity and Robert Johnson were featured speakers—this from a city that, only a few years before, had refused to allow him on their tennis courts because of his skin color. Ashe told the crowd: "Ten years ago this would not have happened. It is as much a tribute to Richmond and the state of Virginia as it is to me."

SECOND LIEUTENANT

ASHE

*A*t UCLA, Ashe was required to join the Reserve Officers' Training Corps (ROTC). This meant that after finishing school he was required to serve two years as an officer in the military. In June 1966, Ashe went to Fort Lewis, Washington, to fulfill his two-year obligation to the military. He was appointed second lieutenant, a responsible position. After boot camp, Ashe was invited to become assistant coach of the Military Academy's tennis team at West Point. However, attending to his job as second lieutenant and working on his game proved to be taxing. Ashe's playing suffered as a result. In 1967, he suffered several embarrassing losses in the Davis Cup action. Military assignments also made him miss several important matches, including Wimbledon in 1966, and the U.S. National Championships in 1967. Still, Ashe ended his military career holding on as the number two player in the nation.

Members of the victorious U.S. Davis Cup team proudly display the honored symbol of the tennis world's highest accomplishment. From left: Arthur Ashe, Donald Dell and Clark Graebner.

Army lieutenant Arthur Ashe holds up his trophy after winning the U.S. Men's Singles Tennis Championship.

BRINGING HOME

THE DAVIS CUP

*A*s 1968 began, Arthur Ashe showed that he could be a contender for the number one spot in tennis. But he had still not captured the top titles in Australia, France, the United States or at Wimbledon. These four tournaments make up the sport's Grand Slam. And changes were happening in the sport that would change Ashe's odds. In 1968, the International Tennis Federation (ITF) gave approval for the first time for amateur and professional tennis players to compete against each other. That meant when Ashe played Wimbledon or the newly created U.S. Open, he would be squaring off against some of the best professional tennis players in the world.

Ashe rose to the challenge and finished number two at Wimbledon. At the Davis Cup match in Cleveland, Ohio, Ashe played some hard-edged tennis in 95-degree heat. After a striking string of tournament victories, he was the top-ranked amateur in the United States. By September 1968, Ashe had 25 wins in a row under his belt. When he won one more time at the U.S. Open men's championship, he became the first African-American man to win a Grand Slam tournament. In December, Ashe led the U. S. Team in the Davis Cup final in Australia. Thanks to victories by Ashe and his teammates, the United States took home the Davis Cup in 1968.

On the way home, the triumphant Davis Cup team passed through 10 countries in Southeast Asia. There, Ashe and his teammates visited U.S. military installations and held tennis exhibitions to entertain the troops stationed there to fight the Vietnam war. The players were hailed as national heroes. President Lyndon Johnson invited them to the White House.

CHIPPING AWAY
AT RACISM

*A*fter the United States team won the Davis Cup, the 25-year-old Ashe attracted the most attention. He was the top-ranked player and the only African-American on the team. Soon his picture appeared on the covers of *Life* magazine, *Sports Illustrated,* and other publications. His name graced Head tennis rackets (the Arthur Ashe Competition) and he signed as a spokesman for a major soft drink company. His years of hard work and dedication to the sport were beginning to pay off in huge financial rewards.

Ashe moved to a swank apartment on New York City's Upper East Side and became one of the world's most eligible bachelor. But because of a sore elbow, Ashe only won two tournaments in 1969.

While Ashe was reaping monetary rewards, he still felt that tennis players were underpaid. The sport had grown by leaps and bounds in the 1960s. Tournaments were drawing huge crowds and televised matches were bringing the sport to millions of people. But the amount of prize money had remained low.

In 1969 Ashe and several other players formed the International Tennis Players Association (ITPA) to protect player's interests. In 1972, the ITPA changed its name to the Association of Tennis Professionals (ATP). The ATP threatened to boycott Wimbledon in 1973 as a protest over the treatment of one of its members. All sides worked out an agreement and Wimbledon proceeded as it had done for almost 100 years.

Arthur Ashe petitioned the General Assembly during a special committee on apartheid. He asked several countries to expel South Africa from the International Lawn Tennis Federation.

From left: musician Quincy Jones, ANC president Nelson Mandela, U.S. activist Randell Robinson and Arthur Ashe all were in South Africa to assess apartheid reforms.

25

In 1969, Ashe applied for a visa to play tennis in South Africa. He was turned down because that country's government had a strict policy of racial segregation called apartheid. It was even worse than what Ashe had experienced growing up in Richmond. Ashe held a press conference and called on the U. S. Lawn Tennis Association, the South African Lawn Tennis Association, and the ITF to protest South Africa's racial policies. As a result of Ashe's actions, South Africa was banned from the Davis Cup competition in 1970. But Ashe did not want to punish individual tennis players in South Africa, just the government.

Ashe brought the South African apartheid issue to the world's attention for the first time. It would take many, many years, but after Ashe's initial protest, the walls of apartheid slowly began to crumble in South Africa.

Ashe never let up on South Africa. As late as 1985, Ashe was arrested at one of the many antiapartheid demonstrations at the South African Embassy in Washington, D.C.

In 1970, the U.S. government asked Ashe to serve as a goodwill ambassador. He toured the African countries of Kenya, Nigeria, Tanzania, and Uganda. Ashe met with heads of state, university students, and ambassadors. In 1971, he toured Cameroon, Gabon, Senegal, and the Ivory Coast.

In Cameroon, Ashe noticed a young tennis player named Yannick Noah who showed a remarkable talent. Ashe arranged to send Noah to France for further training. By the age of 20, Noah had become France's number one tennis player.

In 1973 Ashe was finally granted a visa to play in South Africa. The government realized that if it wanted to participate in the 1976 Olympics, it would have to change its racial policies.

Ashe made several demands about his visit there that had never been granted a black person; he refused to play before a segregated audience; he refused to be made an "honorary white man" as had been demanded by the government; and he wanted to go wherever he pleased and say whatever he wanted. The government gave in to Ashe's demands.

Ashe's trip started a controversy among many blacks in the United States. Some said that by playing there at all, he was saying that the South African government was not so bad. Others said he should worry more about the problems of American blacks. Ashe was criticized for helping Yannick Noah instead of an American tennis player.

"My own case is complicated by the fact that I'm the only one," Ashe said. "I am *the* black tennis player, a bloc by myself. The predicament I'm in is that if I don't spread out my assistance, people become upset. I become the bad guy and I can't win."

Nonetheless, when Ashe played in South Africa's Open in 1973, he became the first black person to compete in that event.

BIG HOLLOW MIDDLE SCHOOL
LEARNING CENTER
34699 N. HIGHWAY 12
INGLESIDE, IL 60041

Chapter 4

Wimbledon

and

Beyond

As the 1975 season began, Ashe's game had been steadily slipping. He had played 123 tournaments between 1971 and 1974 and had won only 11 of them. People thought that he was spending too much time with the ATP, which he was president of, and not enough time on his game. A new generation of talented players like Bjorn Borg and Jimmy Connors had come into the limelight. Experts began to think that the 31-year-old Ashe was past his prime.

Ashe had slipped to number five, but he was not about to give up without a fight. He analyzed the new players and saw that they hit so hard he could never outslug them. His new strategy was to outsmart them. He also pounded his body into shape with a strict weight-training regimen.

By the time Wimbledon began on June 23, Ashe was in fine form. After buzzing through many opponents, Ashe finally faced off against the red-hot Jimmy Connors. Connors, a 22-year-old southpaw from Illinois, was taking the tennis world by storm. In 1974, he had won the U.S. Open, the Australian Open, and 12 other tournaments. At Wimbledon he looked unbeatable.

Arthur Ashe holds his trophy after he beat
Jimmy Connors at Wimbledon.

TENNIS THE MENACE

*A*nd this match was a grudge match. Only days before the match, Connors had slapped Ashe with a $3 million lawsuit, charging him with libel. Ashe had publicly criticized Connors for refusing to play for the United States on the Davis Cup team. Ashe said Connors was "seemingly unpatriotic." Connors was also one of the few top players who refused to join the ATP, Ashe's player's association. Connors showed his displeasure with the organization by filing three lawsuits against the ATP totaling $20 million.

The media was playing up the rivalry between Connors and Ashe. Ashe was billed as the handsome gentleman and Connors as the bad boy of tennis. Connors earned the title by showing abusive and childlike behavior on and off the court. He screamed at linesmen and made obscene gestures at spectators. At Wimbledon the crowds were solidly behind Ashe.

Ashe used his strategy to perfection, keeping Connors on the defense and off-balance. After a grueling match Ashe smashed home the winning point. The crowd roared as Ashe raised his fist in victory. It was one of the most emotional moments of his life. He said later: "When I took the match point, all the years, all the effort, all the support I had received over the years came together. It's a long way from Brookfield to Wimbledon."

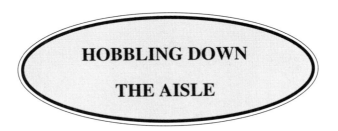

HOBBLING DOWN THE AISLE

*A*fter the win at Wimbledon, Ashe's career was dominated by a slew of younger and stronger opponents. While he still played some impressive games, his numbers began to slip.

While his game was slipping, Ashe's personal life was improving. He met professional photographer Jeanne Marie Moutoussamy in New York City at a fund-raising event. Moutoussamy's assignment for the day was Arthur Ashe. After the photographs were clicked, Ashe asked Jeanne for a date and the two hit it off. After a year of dating, interrupted by 11 months of on-the-road-off-the-road tennis tournaments, the two were married.

Ashe had decided to have bone chips removed from his heel 10 days before the wedding. When he and Jeanne were married February 20, Ashe had to hobble down the aisle in a cast.

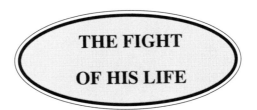

THE FIGHT OF HIS LIFE

*W*ith Ashe's on-court performances on the decline, several of the companies that he represented decided to drop him. He signed on with *Tennis* magazine and wrote a series of articles analyzing the styles of the top players.

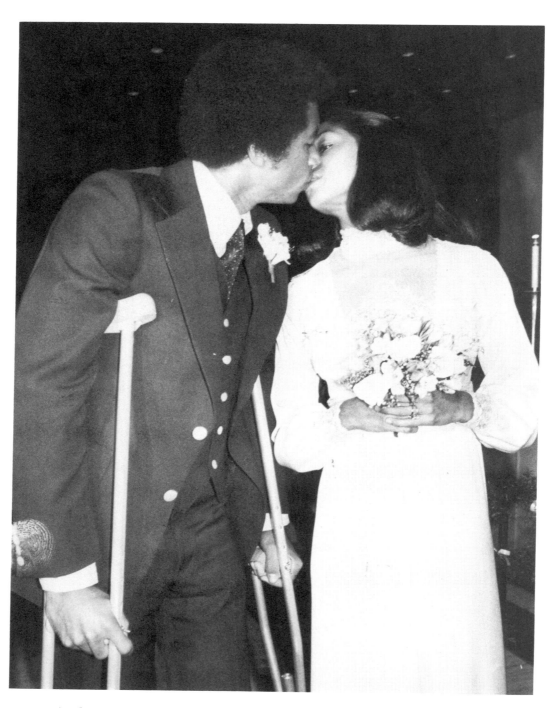

Arthur Ashe kisses his bride, Jeanne Marie Moutoussamy,
after their wedding at the UN Chapel in 1977.

In 1979 Ashe competed in a total of 13 tournaments, and reached the finals in two of them. He was hoping for one more big win before retiring, but it slipped from his grasp. In the middle of the year, however, Ashe was suddenly fighting for something more than a tennis title.

On the morning of July 30, 1979, Ashe woke up with a powerful throbbing pain in his chest. He had just returned home from Wimbledon where he had been eliminated in the first round. "The pain jolted me out of bed," wrote Ashe. "I noticed that the two little fingers on both hands felt 'funny,' as if they had gone to sleep."

The pain stopped and Ashe went back to bed. Fifteen minutes later, the pain returned. Again the pain stopped. Again it returned. Finally the pain stopped. Ashe put the pain out of his mind and went to teach a morning tennis clinic in the Bronx. In the afternoon, he went to another tennis clinic. After signing autographs, Ashe doubled over with searing pain. He tried to wait it out, but this time it would not stop.

A doctor on the scene persuaded Ashe to go to New York Hospital with him immediately. The doctor told him he was having a heart attack. Ashe was shocked. He could not understand how a well-trained professional athlete could have a heart attack at the age of 36. But his father had had two heart attacks. And his mother had died very young, partially because of a weak heart.

Two of the arteries in Ashe's heart were blocked. Doctors told him he would be severely handicapped and would never play tennis again unless he had open-heart surgery. Several months later, Ashe checked into the hospital for a coronary bypass operation. It was a complicated operation, where veins are removed from a patient's leg and sewn into the heart muscle. These new veins allow blood to be pumped by the heart without blockage.

Ashe later wrote: "The two great moments in my life were the day I married Jeannie and the morning I woke up alive: after surgery." But Ashe's days on the tennis court were over. He called a press conference on April 16, 1980, and publicly announced his retirement.

LIFE AFTER TENNIS

As he still played tennis for fun and found a new scope to the game—on the sidelines. He was made captain of the U.S. Davis Cup team and coached many tennis greats. Ashe coached the team to victory, winning the Davis Cup for the United States in 1981 and 1982. By 1984, the clashing personalities and unsportsmanlike behavior of Jimmy Connors and John McEnroe who played for the United States caused Ashe to resign.

In 1985, Arthur Ashe was officially inducted into the Tennis Hall of Fame in Newport, Rhode Island. He won his first amateur title at the age of 12 and finished up his career with a record of 818-260. He had also won 51 of the 304 tournaments he entered.

But tennis no longer defined the life of Arthur Ashe. His daughter Camera Elizabeth was born in 1987 and Ashe was a loving and devoted father to his child. Ashe also joined the fight against heart disease, serving as campaign chairman for the American Heart Association. Ashe helped raise millions of dollars for the organization.

Ashe also helped raise money for the United Negro College Fund and the Safe Passage Foundation, which operates tennis centers in four inner cities. Ashe worked with the African American Athletic Association, which helps disadvantaged athletes in big cities.

Ashe was a talented author. He wrote several tennis instruction books and penned several autobiographies. They are: *Advantage Ashe* (1967), *Arthur Ashe: Portrait in Motion* (1975), *Mastering Your Tennis Stroke* (1976), *Arthur Ashe's Tennis Clinic* (1981), and *Off the Court* (1981).

Ashe received honorary degrees from Dartmouth College, Le Moyne College, Princeton University, St. John's University, and Virginia Union University.

In 1983, the Florida Memorial College asked Ashe to teach a course entitled "The Black Athlete in Contemporary Society." Ashe discovered that there were very few books about black athletes. With the resolve he formerly uses on the tennis court, Ashe set about writing a complete history of black athletics. The job took five years, and when it was over, Ashe had written a massive, ground-breaking study of black American sports. It was released as a three-volume set called *A Hard Road to Glory*.

STRUCK DOWN BY AIDS

*O*n April 8, 1992, Ashe called a press conference. Rumors had been circulating for years and Ashe had to go public with the terrible truth. During a second heart operation in 1983, Ashe had received a blood transfusion tainted with the AIDS virus. Ashe discovered this himself in 1988 when an infection was found in his brain. Further brain surgery revealed that the infection was caused by the AIDS virus.

Tennis great Arthur Ashe pauses while reading a statement
at a news conference where he announced he is HIV positive.
His wife Jeanne looks on.

Ashe had kept the news secret for three years, though some reporters knew about it. At the emotional news conference, Ashe stated: "Any earlier admission of the AIDS infection would have seriously, permanently and unnecessarily infringed upon our family's right to privacy."

Ashe made the announcement only weeks after another major sports figure, Earvin "Magic" Johnson told the world that he, too, had AIDS.

After Ashe announced that he had the disease, he used the media attention to create the Arthur Ashe Foundation for the Defeat of AIDS. In three months, the organization raised $500,000 toward its goal of $5 million by the end of 1993.

Like all the other fights of his life, Ashe refused to let the AIDS virus conquer him. He kept up his demanding schedule of meetings, ceremonies, and fund-raisers. He continued to bound up steps two at a time and had a hearty appetite. Reporters who were following him around to write stories had trouble keeping up with him. But in the end, the AIDS virus beat Arthur Ashe. On February 2, 1993, Ashe checked into New York Hospital with pneumonia. He died at 3:13 p.m. on February 6. He was 49 years old. His wife Jeanne said: "He fought hard, and as in his tennis days, it was always how he played the game."

Arthur Ashe, the skinny kid with glasses and a too-big tennis racket, was buried in Richmond, Virginia. A four-car motorcade brought him to his final resting place. He was not expected so soon.

Arthur Ashe, tennis champion and fighter for human rights.

GLOSSARY

American Tennis Association (ATA)—an African-American tennis organization.

Arteries—blood vessels that bring blood from or away from the heart.

Apartheid—a system of racial segregation in South Africa. Under apartheid black people are separated from white people by law with a set of strict and complicated rules.

Central Intercollegiate Athletic Association—an athletic organization of black colleges.

Coronary bypass— a medical procedure that brings blood to the heart by going around, or bypassing, blocked arteries.

Davis Cup Team—a tennis team made up of the best tennis players in a country. Every country has its own Davis Cup Team.

Segregate—to separate. In the South, laws kept black people segregated from white people.

U. S. Lawn Tennis Association (USLTA)—a national tennis organization.

INDEX

AIDS - 35, 37
American Heart Association - 34
Apartheid - 26
Arthur Ashe Day - 18
Ashe, Arthur, Sr. - 6
Ashe, Camera - 34
Ashe, Jeanne - 31, 34, 37
Ashe, John - 7
Association of Tennis Professionals - 23, 28, 30
Balboa Bay Club - 15
Brookfield Park - 6, 8, 30
Charity, Ronald - 8, 9, 11, 14, 18
Connors, Jimmy - 4, 28, 30, 34
Davis Cup - 17-19, 22, 23, 26, 30, 34
Gibson, Althea - 9
Heart attack - 33
Johnson Award - 17
Johnson, Dr. Robert Walter - 9, 10, 18
Johnson, President Lyndon - 22
Junior Developement Team - 9, 10
Libel suit - 30
Life magazine - 23
McEnroe, John - 34
Morgan, J.D. - 13-15
Noah, Yannick - 26, 27
ROTC - 19
Segregation - 8, 15, 26, 27
South Africa - 26
Sports Illustrated - 23
Tennis Hall of Fame - 34
UCLA - 12, 14, 15, 18, 19
United Negro College Fund - 35
U.S. Nationals - 17-19
U.S. Open - 22
Wimbeldon - 4, 16-19, 22, 23, 28, 30, 31, 33